When the Root Children Wake Up

Retold by AUDREY WOOD

Paintings by NED BITTINGER

SCHOLASTIC INC.

New York Toronto London Auckland Sydney
Mexico City New Delhi Hong Kong Buenos Aires

Old Grandfather Winter slowly walks across the land. He knows that spring will soon be here. Climbing the mountain to his palace of ice, he turns to watch the snows melting behind him.

In her home beneath the ground, Mother Earth lights a fire in the hearth, sweeps away the cobwebs, then throws open the shutters.

Young Robin Redbreast lands at the window.

"Root Children! Root Children!" Young Robin calls. "Wake up! It's time for the masquerade!"

Awakening from their long winter's nap, they stretch and yawn and run their fingers through their tangled hair.

But when they tumble from their beds, all they have to wear are their dreary husk clothes.

"Don't cry," Mother Earth says as she leans out her window and gathers bits of rainbow from the sky. With scissors, needle, and thread, the Root Children set to work making their blossom costumes.

When their costumes are finished, they are laid aside, for there is one task yet to be done. Deep beneath the ground, the Root Children awaken the bugs and lead them up through tunnels lit by fireflies.

Dipping their brushes into the rainbow, the Root Children paint the bugs until they sparkle like jewels.

"It's time to get dressed, Children," Mother Earth calls. "Everyone is waiting."

At last they are ready. Mother Earth unbolts the door then blows upon her horn. "Let the masquerade begin!" she calls.

Dressed in their flowering costumes, the Root Children and jewel-colored bugs rush out into the world. Animals of every kind are there to greet them.

"Wake up, Aunt Spring,"
Young Robin calls.
"The Root Children are here."
Kind Aunt Spring rises
from her bed of ferns and lilies.
The Root Children smother her
with kisses.

"You are so beautiful," kind
Aunt Spring says. "May love
and happiness follow
wherever you may bloom."

The Root Children scatter throughout the land and the air is perfumed with their sweet scent.

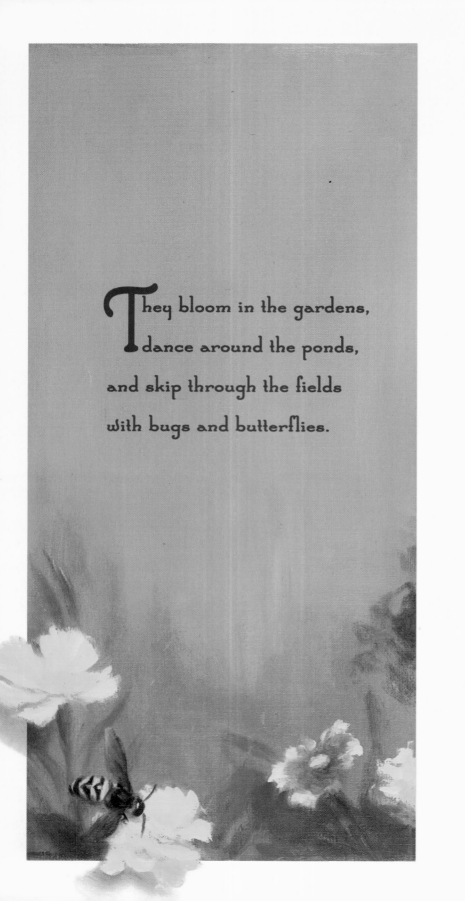

They bloom in the gardens,
dance around the ponds,
and skip through the fields
with bugs and butterflies.

Every day the sun grows warmer, and the Root Children play later. Soon Aunt Spring grows weary from the heat. She returns to her bed of ferns and lilies, closes her eyes, and falls asleep.

Suddenly, jolly Cousin Summer slides down a waterfall and lands with a splash! The Root Children race to greet him, as he shakes the water from his fiery beard.

The weeks pass by, and every sunny day is filled with laughter, music, and dance. It seems as if the masquerade will never end.

But wait. SHHHH. Listen. Studious Uncle Fall is quieting the land. He puts on his spectacles, arranges his pencils and books, then sits down at his desk.

Cousin Summer slips his knapsack on his back and quickly strides over the hills and far away.

A chilling wind begins to blow, and brightly colored leaves whirl to the ground. The wind rips away the Root Children's costumes, leaving only their dreary husk clothes.

Now, once again, Mother Earth blows her horn. "Come home, Root Children," she calls. "Come home. Come home."

In the meadows, gardens, and forests, the Root Children hear her call. One by one they return to their home beneath the ground.

other Earth bolts the door and latches the shutters tightly. The masquerade is over. It is time for her children to dream again. Tucking them in for their long winter's nap, she kisses each one good night. As they drift off to sleep, Mother Earth picks up her lute and sings them a lullaby. . . .

Root Children Sleep

For Edwina Roy—A.W.

To Joan Kindig and the children of Hollymeade—N.B.

Special thanks to: Maggie Stevaralgia, Karen Van Rossem, Julia Masters, William W. Hess, Michael Patrick Hearne, Libby Tucker, J.D. Stahl, Anne Pellowski, and Christian Brassel for their help in our exhaustive search for information about the author and the origins of this story. We were unable to identify a root tale, and we believe this to be an original story by Sibylle von Olfers.

Sibylle von Olfers (1881–1916) wrote and illustrated the original version of *When the Root Children Wake Up*, which was published in 1906 in Germany as *Etwas von den Wurzelkindern* and was illustrated in the art nouveau style. Early in her life, Ms. von Olfers received drawing lessons. By the time she reached eighteen, she had become a nun and continued her art studies. To help herself learn art, she copied the Italian masters. She created some religious artwork, and several of these pieces have been preserved in the Herz-Jezu-Kirche in Lübeck, Germany. She wrote and illustrated ten picture books, but her masterpiece was her charming story about the Root Children, which has been beloved by children for generations. And now, after nearly one hundred years, the story is reborn.